MARTHA SPEAKS™

Meet Martha

Written by Karen Barss

Based on the characters created by Susan Meddaugh

HOUGHTON MIFFLIN HARCOURT

Boston • New York • 2010

Martha Speaks
Picture Clue Key

alphabet soup

letters

burger

Martha

bus

paint

family

pizza

flower

telephone

Helen

garden

For information about permission to reproduce selections from this book, write to Permissions, Houghton Mifflin Harcourt Publishing Company, 215 Park Avenue South, New York, New York 10003.

Library of Congress Cataloging-in-Publication Data is on file.

ISBN 978-0-547-21079-7

Design by Bill Smith Group.

www.hmhbooks.com
www.marthathetalkingdog.com

Manufactured in China / LEO 10 9 8 7 6 5 4 3 2 1
4500210424/4500210450 (pb)

Meet Martha.

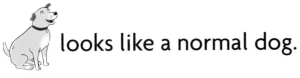 looks like a normal dog.

She likes to dig in the .

And she likes to dig in the trash!

 likes to be petted and scratched.

She loves to eat.

Did you know can order a 🍔?

Yes, 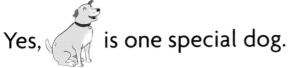 is one special dog.

She can talk!

How is that possible?

One day  ate  .

The  went to her brain, not her tummy.

Then  spoke!

Hello! When's dinner?

Martha's  was very surprised!

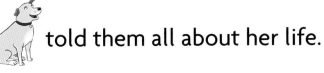 told them all about her life.

Finally, she could tell them what she was thinking!

 and are best friends.

More brown.
Looks like bacon.
Yum!

 likes to draw and ✐ .

🐕 gives 🧍 advice.

Helen's mom works in a  shop.

Sometimes helps out.

Helen's dad drives a .

 chats and keeps him company.

Helen's little brother is Jake.

 is helping him learn to speak.

Martha's brother is Skits, who does not talk.

So tells the what his barks mean.

But sometimes  talks too much!

She ordered  on the  . . .

I was going to share . . .

then her  found out!

Sometimes  surprises people.

Words can be fun.
Words can also be very useful.

Words helped when was in the dog

shelter without her collar.

And one time,  even stopped a burglar!

Her was very proud.

 is one lucky dog. She can speak!

And her family loves her very much.

Story Picture Cards

Punch out the cards and use them as either flash cards or story picture starters. For the story picture game, take three to five cards and lay them on the table. Young readers can have fun using the new vocabulary words in that order to tell an original story. Mix them up and do it again!